For Mike, Katy and Kit—with all my love
—J.B.
For Gillian
—S.M.

Library of Congress Cataloging-in-Publication Data
Blatt, Jane.
Books always everywhere / Jane Blatt ; illustrated by Sarah Massini. —
First American edition.
   p.   cm.
Summary: A celebration of the many ways children interact with books.
ISBN 978-0-385-37506-1 (trade) — ISBN 978-0-375-98205-7 (ebook)
[1. Stories in rhyme. 2. Books and reading—Fiction.]   I. Massini, Sarah, ill. II. Title.
PZ8.3.B5972Bo 2013   [E]—dc23   2013006566

MANUFACTURED IN CHINA
10 9 8 7 6 5 4 3 2 1
First American Edition

BOOKS
Always Everywhere

Jane Blatt
Illustrated by
Sarah Massini

Random House
New York

Book big

elephant

Book small

Book wide

"Hello," said Mr. Croc

Mommy
and Me

Book tall

Book build

Book mat

Book
chair

Book
hat

Daft Hats

Sitting Pretty

I'm the
King
of the
castle

WUTHERING HEIGHTS

100 BEST HIGH CHAIRS

Book park

THE
THREE
LITTLE
PIGS

CINDERELLA
CINDERELLA
CINDERELLA
CINDERELLA
CINDERELLA
CINDERELLA
CINDERELLA
CINDERELLA
DERELLA
LLA

Little Red Riding Hood

KS

BOOK

BOOK

Book
shop

Book start

Book stop

Book
scary

Book
funny

PEEK-A-BOO!

A peephole book
to make you giggle
and chortle and chuckle
and roar with laughter

100 JUNGLE JOKES

SILLY BILLY

banana

Book rainy

In sunshine
or in rain,
every day is
a story day.

Happy
Days

Book sunny

Book give

Book share

Books always . . .

. . . every

where.